# SENTIENT CLAUS

*A Sentient Object Holiday Romance*

## Holly Wilde

# CONTENTS

# PREFACE

Indie author life comes with being active on socials in order to self promote our material. While connecting with readers and authors is seriously one of the coolest things about writing, the constant attacks towards provocative content can be draining. Online harassment and bullying are sadly common in many communities, including the bookish world of social media. So, naturally, I turned what I was witnessing into the story you're holding in your hands.

Purity culture and religious moral values can be deeply harmful and trigger strong emotional responses. In a patriarchal society, these puritanical norms foster misogyny, where people—especially women—are judged based on their sexual choices. This can result in slut shaming, eroding self-esteem and autonomy.

In *Sentient Claus,* I explore purity culture while parodying the stereotypical chronically online male. By turning a beloved male figure, Santa, into an asshole, I critique the harmful rhetoric that is often shared online with my own brand of absurdity.

My goal with this book is to commiserate with others who see and experience the hatred spouted in our spaces, while adding humor and nonsensical dialogue and events. However, I realize that, although this is a funny story, the subject matter approached is real and traumatic to many.

Other considerations to take in that may be uncomfortable for some readers includes:

-Purity Culture
(Exploration of societal expectations regarding sexual behavior, particularly regarding women's purity and virtue.)

-Misogynist Male Lead
(A portrayal of a male character who embodies misogynistic attitudes and beliefs.)

-Slut Shaming
(Depictions of judgment and criticism directed at individuals for their sexual choices.)

-Online Harassment
(Scenes that include harassment and bullying in digital spaces.)

-Femme Domme Dynamics
(Elements of female dominance in sexual

relationships, including power exchanges.)

-Cock Caging and Anal Toys
 (Graphic descriptions of sexual practices that may be explicit or uncomfortable for some readers.)

-Dubious Consent (Dubcon)
 (Situations involving unclear or questionable consent.)

-Double Penetration and Humiliation

(Graphic and explicit depictions of sexual acts and themes of humiliation.)

For those with past trauma related to these topics, these portrayals may be particularly distressing. Reader discretion is strongly advised.

# SENTIENT CLAUS

# CHAPTER ONE

"I gotta be honest," Blitzen whispers, the words forming puffy clouds in the evening air. "I think we're gonna be home in record time this year."

"Shh," Donder snaps, casting a quick glance over his shoulder. "He'll hear us."

"Let him," Cupid dares the rest of the reindeer. "It's not like we don't already know. The workshop elves can't keep a secret to save their lives."

Donder fires back a quick retort in an attempt to put an end to the conversation. "I know, but he's been in a foul mood for weeks. Nothing that the missus does is snapping him out of it, and I'm not about to poke the bear. I suggest you don't either."

Sylas strains to hear the hushed conversations drifting from the front of the line, but the wind keeps snatching up bits of information before it can reach him. It's the night before Christmas Eve, and Sylas, the North Pole's only sleigh, waits for the sun to finish setting so the Christmas Team can make their final practice run. Tension crackles through the reindeer ahead of him, though Sylas has no clue why.

Normally, he's one of the first to be in the loop, privy to all the gossip from both the elves and the animals. But tonight, as he stares at the snow-dusted backends of Blitzen and Donder, something feels off. Secrets swirl around them with the blizzard, but no one's willing to share what's going on. It stings more than the biting cold that they're leaving him sidelined. Sure, the reindeer love their games, but they've never shut him out like this. Deciding to take a chance, Sylas tries to get the attention of his reindeer friends.

"Psst," the hiss over his speakers cuts through the silent night as he talks. "Can someone tell me what's going on with Santa?"

"I'll tell you what the fuck is going on with Santa," Santa's booming voice rumbles through the night like a cannon blast. Startled, the reindeer jump, their hooves levitating off the ground briefly before settling back onto the runway. Santa appears behind them, clomping through the snow in jeans and a red fleece pullover. "Erotica, Sylas. That's my fucking problem. Salacious smut is the latest craze, and it's affecting the numbers on *The Lists*." Santa's eyes darken as he looks over the horizon. "There won't be as many stops this year, and it's all because readers today prefer to dive into a book about ho ho ho's rather than enjoy a good, old-fashioned novel."

Sylas is baffled by the idea that stories are the source of Santa's anger. Of all things, books seem like the least likely culprit. "Is there a big Naughty List this year?"

Santa nods, his rosy cheeks blotchy and his expression unusually grim. "Oh, it's not just big, it's a goddamned crisis! I hate to admit it, but there's been a sixty-nine percent jump in names moving from the Nice List to the Naughty List.

The humans don't want the warmth of the season, they want *heat* and *spice*. The whole genre of romance has turned into...well, let's just say it's graphic content. They've even come up with silly little names to differentiate between the types, like romantasy, but I know the truth. No matter how they dress it up, they're nothing more than vapid little bits of trash."

Sylas asks, "But aren't they just stories?

"Absolutely not! Look, Sylas, you're a wonderful sleigh, but you don't understand those kinds of...urges." He practically spits the word out, like it's poison. Santa pinches the bridge of his nose, the exasperation rolling off of him in waves. "These books taint the very idea of love. And people are consuming them faster than I can scarf down cookies left beside the tree. The thought of going down a chimney and being greeted by shelves full of that filth makes my stomach turn. I can't bear it.

What's worse is they don't even advertise their shameful deeds. Now, the novels come with cartoon illustrations on the front, making it more discreet when people pull the paperbacks from their bags out in public. At least back in the day they would have to tote around covers that scream out *I'm a pervert*, with bare chested men, their wild, roguish hair blowing in the wind.

Back then, the offenders would have to deal with whispers, looks, and maybe even some pointed fingers. Now, they get no consequences for their choices. I've had enough of them parading the prose of promiscuity, which is why I'm making things right this Christmas. I've put them *all* on the Naughty List this year. Smut writers and readers alike. Maybe that'll teach them to seek their own happily ever after with a monogamous partner in real life instead of relying on fictional happy endings."

The reindeer and sleigh have never witnessed him this worked up, especially not over what's going on down south with the humans. Santa's so heated that his forehead is covered with a sheen of sweat, like he's just dunked his head in a melted puddle of snow. His impassioned speech sends a violent shiver through the reins as the reindeer shift uncomfortably in their harnesses.

Sylas wants to comfort Santa, assuring him it can't be that bad, but the expression on his face stops him in his tracks. Santa's the opposite of holly and jolly—he's moody and irritable. His arms cross over his strong, broad chest, and his thin lips are pursed in a scowl, like he's ready to snap at anyone who approaches. If body language could talk, Santa's would be screaming that this smut-tastrophe is no joke.

Santa heaves himself into the sleigh, his hunk of a dad-bod settling awkwardly on the red satin bench. He quickly fastens the seatbelt, but to Sylas, it lacks the usual spirit. Instead of laughter making his belly jiggle, it merely squishes down as they prepare for departure.

Grabbing the worn, burgundy leather reins, Santa gives the pre-flight instructions, "Now Dasher, now Dancer, now Prancer, now... Oh, fuck it. Let's ride, ladies!"

Without hesitation, the reindeer move in unison. Powdery snow tickles Sylas' undercarriage as they launch from a trot to a full run. They have five hundred feet of runway, but it only takes twenty to soar into the sky. For anyone else, the wintery weather would make takeoff impossible, but for Sylas and the reindeer, it's second nature.

Santa's Christmas Team was handpicked for their unique talents to ensure the success of the annual gift delivery. Each reindeer was chosen for their unmatched speed and agility in even the toughest winter storms. But the true marvel is Santa's sentient sleigh. He wasn't born, he was made. Carefully crafted by the North Pole's finest elven artisans, Sylas was meticulously forged and enchanted by powerful magic. His purpose is to carry Santa and his sack of presents through the night skies, delivering joy to the world. But he's not just any sleigh; he can think. His brilliant mind can make split-second decisions like changing course when needed.

He can also *feel*. And right now, he's saddened by the thought that this holiday season won't be what it once was. With Christmas Eve just hours away, Sylas shifts his focus to finding a solution. Afterall, being a sleigh makes him great at maneuvering around obstacles. The only difference now is that he's dodging moral dilemmas instead of chimneys and rooftops. Questions flood his mind, demanding answers he's not prepared to face.

*Will Christmas be canceled?*

*What will happen to the workshop if no one gets presents?*

*What will become of him if no one needs a sleigh ride through the stars?*

Instead of overwhelming Santa with a barrage of concerns, Sylas narrows his focus to a single question. "How do we fix this?"

Santa leans back, and the familiar weight of him settling into Sylas' seat quiets the sleigh's racing thoughts. "I don't know, buddy. That's what's been keeping me up at night."

Sylas notices the melted snowflakes on Santa's cheek, and wonders if some of them are actually tears. Silence stretches between them as they soar through the night. Stars shimmer like glitter peaking through the clouds as the darkness spreads wide and endless above. Below, the world is blanketed in stillness, rooftops dusted with snow, and glowing windows dotting the landscape. They coast through the air in contemplative quiet, until Santa shares his secret to Sylas.

"I've got these anonymous social media accounts where I comment on naughty posts. Lately, I've been targeting these bookish influencers and authors, calling out what they're really reading—porn for lonely losers.

It's not like my points aren't valid. When I earnestly ask, 'What happened to good books?' and 'Who's letting this shit get published?', these people get so defensive. My notifications pop off with some crap about patriarchy and misogyny, or calling me a troll. Which is ridiculous because I'm clearly part elf, not a troll.

I've spent months trying to explain that reading is really cheating, but they all just double down on their fantasy characters. Trust me, I've tried to open the eyes of that community, but the indie book situation seems too big to control. Maybe there's no fixing it. Maybe I'm too late."

Sylas glides silently through the night, lost in thought. He never expected Santa to turn his bench into a confessional. An unsettling realization creeps in, tugging on Sylas' awareness. What Santa admitted doesn't sit right. It almost sounds like his friend has been harassing people simply for loving certain stories. But that couldn't be—harassment is Naughty List behavior. If these books have driven Santa to do such a thing, Sylas wonders how dangerous romance can be.

The laughter and chatter of years past are

replaced by the rush of wind and the distant sound of water splashing over icebergs. The reindeer's heads hang low, not daring to break the awkward silence stretching between Santa and his loyal sleigh. Even their bells ring softer, as if they're trying to fly as quietly as possible. Sylas glances back, hoping Santa will say something, anything, but the bearded man is locked in his own bitterness. Yet, as they fly on, Sylas can't shake the smut situation from his mind. It's obviously important, and he's determined to help.

It's times like these that Sylas wishes the magic that brought him to life had also given him arms and legs. Afterall, he's just a sleigh—he can't simply find a book that's corrupting the world and grab it off the shelf.

Or... can he?

# CHAPTER TWO

The reindeer guide them through the night as though on autopilot. Sylas focuses on the steady jingling of their bells while mentally running through his plan over and over again. It's going to be dangerous, but there's only one way to uncover the facts, and that's breaking into Santa's office.

After every practice flight, Santa always heads for a debrief with the elves and then takes a shower before settling in for his pre-Christmas nap. That's Sylas' window of opportunity. The workshop will be a flurry of activity, with elves darting every which way to check inventory, wrap gifts, and sip cocoa before the final Christmas push. Sylas hopes that amidst the frenzy of the holiday rush, no one will notice him sneaking around.

The lists should be on Santa's desk, ready for tomorrow's last-minute checks. Santa's always meticulous about documenting even the tiniest details, so if smut is the problem, Sylas bets the titles will be neatly listed next to the offenders. All he has to do is choose one and confront whatever darkness lurks within those pages. If Sylas is going to understand how to dismantle the entire romance genre and make Christmas cozy once more, he needs to read an erotic novella.

Glowing lights from the North Pole finally appear in the distance. Santa's sprawling workshop comes into view, its thousands of vibrant string lights twinkling like a galaxy of stars. Normally, this would be a cheerful sight, but tonight, coming home brings a mix of anticipation and anxiety.

They land smoothly onto the tarmac, a light dusting of snow kicking up around Sylas' runners. Santa dismounts with a grunt, his boots crunching on the arctic white as he steps down. Without a word, he turns away, leaving Sylas with a pang of sadness. Starting the season on the wrong ski weighs heavy on him, but he convinces himself he's making the right choice. Yes, breaking and entering is Naughty List behavior, but Santa's broken heart is arguably worse.

Santa pauses by Sylas's sloping backside and gives the wood a gentle pat before trudging toward the workshop doors. His head is high, but his shoulders curve with defeat as he shuffles beneath the flickering candy-cane-striped street lamps. The reindeer nervously glance back at Sylas before taking off to the stables.

Sylas watches as Santa disappears into the bustling crowd of elves. This is it—it's officially go time. Not wanting to make it obvious that he's straying from his post-flight routine, he glides toward the garage. Before sliding inside the inviting warmth, he slips into the shadows that cling to the exterior of the brick building. Santa's office is in a different wing, and the hallways connecting the buildings are too narrow for him to fit.

Frantically searching for a way inside, he rounds the corner and finds a delivery door left slightly ajar. But to reach it, he'll have to cross a well-lit expanse and hope he isn't spotted. Steeling himself for the challenge, he drives off. The only evidence of his daring mission are the two sleigh tracks already vanishing under the rapidly falling snow.

Squeezing his ample frame inside isn't exactly easy, but with a bit of maneuvering, he manages to slip into the workshop without drawing attention. The clatter of hammers and saws drowns out any sound he might make as Sylas navigates through the chaos. He's focused on one goal, getting to Santa's office.

Peeking around a corner, Sylas spots the large, frosted glass double doors looming ahead, softly glowing from the warm light within. His runners glide effortlessly over the red-and-white checkered floor, only offering the occasional squeak in quiet protest of his criminal activity. From the conference suite next door, he hears the muffled sounds of Santa's debriefing. The soft rustling of papers and the low murmur of voices are layered beneath the heavy, clunking footsteps of Santa himself. The steady thunk, thunk, thunk, turn makes it obvious that Santa's pacing the room as he delivers instructions to the crew.

It's now or never.

Sylas slips through the office doors, the plush red carpet muffling the sound of his runners as he glides inside. Santa's office is as warm and inviting as ever, the space is brimming with holiday charm. Snow globes, vintage nutcrackers, and evergreen garlands drape over the mantle of a stone fireplace. Old black-and-white photos in ornate frames display centuries of Christmas cheer. The faint smell of cinnamon brandy lingers in the air, mixed in with the sweet scent of pine.

But none of that hold's Sylas' attention for long. He's immediately drawn to the massive oak desk at the center of the room. On top of it, and exactly where he hoped, is the Naughty List, unfurled like a scroll of judgment. The parchment stretches across the desk, its edges curling slightly, and the names permanently etched in a neat, looping script. He inches closer until he can read each name and the notes beside them. Just as he suspected, the titles of the offending books are listed, too.

*All I Want For Christmas is Sex*

*Suck My Mistletoes*

*Wrap It Up For My Box*

Okay, Sylas admits that the titles are overtly sexual, but he also knows better than to judge a book by its cover. It's not like people are publishing stories with giant peens plastered on the front, afterall.

His thoughts are abruptly cut off by the sound of cheerful goodbyes echoing from the conference suite, oblivious to Sylas lurking in the room next door. He freezes, straining his senses as he hears Santa's heavy footsteps lead into the hallway. The door shuts with a thud behind him, and the voices of the elves begin to fade away as the crowd leaves the debriefing. Sylas' entire plan hinges on Santa heading straight to the showers after the meeting.

He sends a silent plea to the stars above, hoping the boss won't have any reason to return to the office. The quiet feels heavier than usual, as if even the magic of the workshop is holding its breath along with him. Lying to Santa is out of the question, so the last thing Sylas needs is to be caught in the act. The faint ticking of the clock on the wall is the only sound breaking the silence, each second dragging on as Sylas waits for Santa to finally shuffle away.

Once the coast is clear, Sylas drifts back to the massive Naughty List, his focus zeroing in on the top baddies. As he scans the names of the worst of the worst, his gaze lands on the number one spot. Ivy Holidaye. An emergency room nurse in her mid-thirties, Ivy spends her days healing the sick and caring for the wounded. Smart, funny, and a good friend, she seems like a perfect candidate for the Nice List. So, why did someone so selfless end up on the Naughty List?

The answer is buried in her secret life. Ivy Holidaye is a fantasy romance writer, and according to Santa's notes, her books are spicier than a hot apple cider on a cold winter's night. Sylas looks at the title of her latest novella, *Frost My Cookie with Pleasure and Pain.* At under fifty pages, it's a quick read, perfect for Sylas to skim through and discover what exactly makes smut so awful. He can't help but wonder what could possibly be so scandalous about cookies or frosting, but he trusts Santa's notes.

With the title committed to memory, Sylas slips out of Santa's office as quietly as he entered. The faint glow of street lamps guides his path as he moves through the snow toward his home in the garage. He slides into his personal spot, the familiar scent of unfinished pine and the sting of acidic varnish welcoming him.

Once parked, Sylas wastes no time searching the internet for *Frost My Cookie with Pleasure and Pain.* The cover pops up on his console screen, a cute illustrated image of a cookie surrounded by whimsical swirls of frosting. At first glance, nothing about it seems scandalous. Except for the way the white icing drips from the text, giving the whole thing a slightly messy and sticky vibe.

With hesitation, Sylas opens the first page. He's immediately met with a list of trigger warnings featuring phrases and abbreviations he's never encountered before. *Words like impact play, consensual sensory deprivation*, and *CEI (cum eating instructional).* His wooden frame stiffens, and a sinking feeling washes over him as he realizes he's about to learn more than he ever wanted to about being naughty.

# CHAPTER THREE

The cold emptiness beside him catches Santa off guard as he stirs, his hand brushing over her untouched side of the mattress. Mrs. Claus hadn't come to bed last night. The tension between them has been simmering for days, ever since she caught him online, exchanging messages with women again.

She was punishing him with her silence, leaving him to wake up alone on his biggest day of the year. Typical. He rolls onto his back and stares up at the ceiling, irritated by the whole situation. It wasn't like he was flirting, he had shown her the messages for Christmas' sake. But somehow reading what he posted only made the irrational woman more upset.

*"It's a shame so many females waste their time on these books. Can't y'all find a hobby?"*

*"Smut like this is why relationships in real life fall apart."*

*"If people spent half the time they waste on this*

*garbage actually doing something worthwhile in this world, then peace on Earth could really exist."*

She hadn't even spoken, just stood there with her arms folded, an unbecoming frown on her face as she read the words on the screen. When he tried to explain how he was fulfilling his job calling out bad behavior and upholding Christmas values, Gertie had simply shaken her head. Then she left, and Santa hasn't seen her since.

He grumbles under his breath, the rumble of his belly echoing the sound. Usually, he's greeted by the scent of peppermint cookies, freshly brewed coffee, and gooey cinnamon rolls, all courtesy of Mrs. Claus. He could really go for a decent breakfast to wake him up, but something tells him the kitchen is as empty as his belly. The house is disturbingly quiet. No clinking of cookie sheets, no humming of festive tunes. No one performing their wifely duties.

Santa checks his watch to find it's only eleven p.m., still December twenty-third despite feeling like he's slept until Christmas Eve. It's too early for her to be making breakfast, but that doesn't mean that she shouldn't have some midnight snacks available for him. With a low, bitter grunt, he tosses the blankets off. It takes effort to sit up, the tension in his broad, muscular back popping as he rubs his eyes and stretches. Swinging his legs over the side of the bed, he shivers at the cold carpet beneath his feet. He doesn't want to get up. He shouldn't have to. Why should he be the one hunting her down when she's the one who took off and is sulking like a child? But,

17

if he doesn't go looking for her, she'll hold it against him later.

The thought grates on him as he forces himself to stand, the biting air nipping at his bare skin. He shuffles across the carpet, each step heavier than the last as his irritation builds. Who ever said *Happy Wife Happy Life* clearly had no clue what the fuck they were talking about.

As he strides toward the bathroom, he catches a faint glow through the frost covered window. The garage light is on, which is odd. It's too early for the sleigh to be prepped, and the reindeer should still be asleep. Something's not right.

*Fantastic, Gertie's probably curled up in the sleigh, freezing in that fucking garage,* he thinks bitterly to himself.

He stumbles to the closet. "Where's my...oh, for the love of fruitcake!" He curses, glaring at the empty space where his clothes are usually laid out. Yet another way the darling missus has decided to screw him over. Santa flounders through the closet, grabbing the first pair of pants he can find. Hopping around haphazardly like an uncoordinated ballerina, he nearly trips over the corner chair while sliding his legs into the red sweatpants.

His socks are on backwards, and he doesn't even bother with underwear. There's no doubt that he's a mess, but it's clear in his mind that his wife is to blame for it all. Yanking a flannel shirt from the closet, he fumbles with the buttons, realizing halfway through that they're misaligned. He scowls but doesn't bother fixing it.

The entire house is empty, no elves, no animals, and no Gertie, just Santa dashing through the halls. Reaching the back door, Santa jams his feet into his boots, barely bothering with the laces as they trail behind him like forgotten reins. The cold snow soaks through the flailing strings, seeping into his boots and making his feet ache as he tears through the expansive yard.

Just as he's halfway across, the night sky above him shifts. His eyes snap upward, and he spots his sleigh swooping in for a landing. Its polished runners gleam under the moonlight as it slices through the air. The sight of Sylas making an unauthorized flight ignites a fire of anger in Santa's chest. Gone are all the thoughts of Mrs. Claus, right now there's only one thing on Santa's mind, and it's figuring out why the sleigh was on the move without getting his permission.

His heart drums a frantic rhythm for his feet to follow as he picks up the pace. By the time he reaches the side of the building, slightly out of breath, he's fuming. Santa throws open the side door with a sharp yank, his hand white-knuckled on the knob as he stomps inside. Snow blows in from the open door, but he doesn't pay attention to the frozen air as he makes his way across the garage. His boots thud on the concrete floor, the sound bouncing off the walls of the cavernous room.

There, sitting stoic as ever, is Sylas. The sleigh is silent, motionless, acting like nothing happened.

But Santa knows everything. He knows that Sylas isn't sleeping. He knows his sleigh's awake. The only thing he doesn't know is how he's going to punish the little shit for disobeying the rules, but as he spies the axe propped up in the corner, he begins to come up with an idea or two.

"I'll give you one chance to answer me truthfully. What the hell do you think you're doing?"

Sylas wobbles for the briefest moment, a wave of guilt rushing over him as he notices Santa's face growing redder than his traditional suit. It feels strange, being on the receiving end of Santa's rage. Sylas wars with himself on whether or not he should divulge the details of what he did. It would be one thing if all he had to do was admit to sneaking away to read a forbidden book. He'd have an easier time explaining that, compared to how he spent the other half of the night. Still, Sylas knows that Santa has eyes everywhere, and he'll find out what's been done one way or another. Better for it to come directly from the sleigh himself than from a third party.

"Well, to start, I went into your office and read the Naughty List. I know it's an invasion of privacy, but I..."

Santa takes a menacing step towards his sleigh, his eyes narrowing in on Sylas as he interrupts, "You've got no business looking at that list. It's confidential and classified."

"I get that, Santa, I do. I just wanted to get a better understanding of what was making

Christmas so troublesome this year."

"I already told you Sylas, it's the popularity of risqué romances. But, it's not your duty to rationalize my decisions. I'll forgive you this time, since I know how you like being helpful. But your only task is to carry the gifts, plain and simple. Stick to that."

There's a tender part of Sylas that seeks Santa's approval, which is why he's nervous to inform his friend that he did indeed stick to his main job, just in a different way.

"Delivering presents is my purpose, Santa. It's who I am." Sylas' voice peals through the speaker on his dash with quiet conviction. "That's why I had to make sure no one was left out. When you saw me land, I was coming back from bestowing cheer to those whose only crime was reading books you disapprove of."

"You did what?!" Santa's face contorts with fury as he growls.

"Don't worry, Santa. I didn't ruin Christmas. I made sure to save the Nice List gifts for tomorrow's ride, just like always."

Santa slams his boot to the ground, his belly quivering like a bowl full of joyless jelly. "What the fuck were you thinking? The Naughty List is bigger than it's ever been, and instead of reinforcing the boundaries that I've set, you're out there celebrating despicable habits! You most certainly *did* ruin Christmas, you stupid fucking pile of junk!"

Sylas is stunned by the insults Santa's hurling

21

at him. He expected anger, maybe even a lecture, but that was a personal attack. He refuses to feel shame for spreading Christmas magic. Santa's words cut deep, but Sylas isn't here to defend himself. He's here to defend the outcasts.

"Santa," he begins, choosing his words carefully, "I understand you think what I did was reckless, and I know you don't agree with my choices. But punishing people for reading? For enjoying stories that bring them comfort or make them feel alive? That goes against what I stand for."

"Indulging in carnal urges is anti-Christmas!"

"If romance is outlawed this year, what will you target next? Thrillers? True crime?"

Santa snorts. "*Those* are actually stories. Romance is straight up porn disguised as intellectual content."

But Sylas knows smut isn't bad. In fact, something stirred within him while reading Ivy Holidaye's book, forever changing the way he understands the world. Now, as he faces Santa's wrath, he realizes that Naughty and Nice are constructs used to divide people. Purity is merely a myth. Santa can't see it, yet, and maybe he never will, but Sylas won't back down.

"You know as well as I do that being Naughty Listed is an extreme punishment, Santa. It's treason to the season, and I won't be an accomplice to your hatred. "

Sylas can see the steam practically radiating from Santa like a boiling kettle. Losing complete control, his words thunder through the garage. "Treason? You, the one who committed numerous crimes in one night, are accusing me of treason? That's rich." Santa scoffs. "I keep it real simple, only good folks get goodies. And romance readers aren't good, they're immoral! You'd be wise to remember that I have the final say on who is good and who is bad. I am the judge. I am the jury. I am Santa Claus, god dammit! And You!" he sticks his finger into Sylas' paneling while yelling at the sleigh, "You've undermined the very essence of Christmas!"

Sylas searches for the words but falters when, for the first time since arriving, he takes a good look at the man before him. He's never seen Santa so disheveled. His buttons are in the wrong holes, his boots are untied, and he's out here in a blizzard without even a hat. Sylas expected a fight with Santa, the formidable figure in the red suit, but now he feels a pang of pity for the man standing before him.

This isn't the all-powerful gift bringer, it's just a guy who berates people online. Just Nick.

Sylas softens his tone as he confronts the heart of the issue. "Are you sure it's about what's right and wrong? Or could you be targeting a genre that's historically loved by women, and disrespecting them over whatever discomfort you feel about sensuality?" Santa bristles, but Sylas continues before he's interrupted. "*Frost My Cookie with Pleasure and Pain*, well it opened my eyes. When the season comes and goes, and you've only given gifts to those you've deemed 'nice,' you'll realize how empty your actions are. Because you're leaving out the people who understand love the most."

For a moment, there's nothing but silence between them. Santa's shoulders rise and fall with heaving breaths. He's tired of listening to the sleigh flaunting its corruption, and he has the perfect mute button. Santa turns sharply on his heel, making his way to the back corner of the garage for the red axe. He grabs it, turning the wooden handle over in his hands to find his grip. Refocusing his attention on Sylas, he glares at his sleigh.

Finally, Santa speaks, his voice low and cold. "I've had enough of your talk, Sylas. As of this moment, you're suspended from the Christmas Team, indefinitely. You will not be joining me for Christmas this year, or any other year. Goodbye, old friend. You don't deserve the honor of flying for the North Pole."

# CHAPTER FOUR

**M**rs. Claus wraps her scarf snugly around her neck and tugs her favorite woolen mittens up, trying to smother the storm building inside her. The windy night nips at her cheeks as she rounds the bend toward the cozy warmth of their house. She thought that taking a walk would calm her down and clear her head, but it only made her more upset. Nick's always been under pressure the closer it gets to Christmas, but things have changed this year. He's distant, brooding, and spending more time listening to men with microphones on those damn podcasts than with her.

Gertie had known something was wrong the moment Nick started spending every night holed up in his office, coming up with excuse after excuse not to spend time with her. "Not now," he'd say while ducking back to his desk yet again. "Don't worry about it, hun. Just go back to the kitchen."

The words stung more every time he said

them. She wasn't just some background decoration, there to stand beside him, smiling while he ran the world. She's supposed to be his partner. At least, she *could* be, if only he'd let her in.

But what she found that night fractured something inside her. Catching him red-handed, typing those vile messages online, she realized he was hiding more than just late-night work. He was attacking the very thing she loved most. Sexy books.

Nick has always been traditional, but seeing the way he puts down romance readers, especially women, makes her stomach twist. His crude comments about smut were harsh and dripping with self-righteous judgment. But worst of all is, Santa has no idea that the stories he's trashing are the very ones she keeps tucked away. If he knew about her stash of steamy romances, would he talk to her in that way? Mrs. Claus has a sinking feeling that the answer is yes, he'd judge her just the same. He'd relish in making her feel small for loving something he disapproves of, and that hurts most of all.

Tears prick her eyes as Gertie pauses mid step and stares at the house. The familiar comfort of the home is gone, replaced by a hollowness, like the magic has been drained from it. She notices a light on in the bedroom, and the thought of climbing into bed with her husband makes Gertrude's stomach drop. Just as she's about to turn back and retrace her steps, a burst of voices shatters the stillness. She recognizes Nick's immediately, loud and thick with anger.

The other voice, though quieter, sounds familiar. She strains to listen, brow furrowing in concentration. *Sylas, it's Sylas.* Curiosity pulls her forward. Carefully, Gertie inches closer to the open side door of the garage, making sure to stay hidden in the shadows, just out of their line of sight. Something is off, she's never heard Nick speak this way to the Christmas Team.

"Now hold on, Santa, don't give me that look!" Sylas' words are sharp. "I know you think there's something wrong with smutty books, but have you ever actually read one of them?"

"Absolutely not! I'm not some punk ass bitch who reads. I just know that romance is Naughty List shit."

Mrs. Claus feels a chill swoop over her, and it's not from the snowstorm at her back. Taking a chance, she peeks around the doorframe, knowing that she's risking exposure, but needing to know if Sylas is safe. Her breath quickens, anger boiling up from somewhere deep inside when she sees Santa twirling the axe in his hands and marching towards the sleigh.

"You thought you were so slick delivering gifts to the naughty, well let me know how you like this Christmas story: We're going to return to each of those houses and take back the presents they never should have received. But that's not all, I plan on confiscating their slutty stories, too. Then, I'm gonna chop you up into kindling, and personally toss those books into a fire made from your burning body!"

All these years, her husband led her to believe he was tirelessly working to keep the world a safe and happy place. It's why she's always been a doting wife, taking care of the home while Santa spreads joy to the world. In actuality, she hasn't been supporting him, she's enabled him. Gertie stood by, silently letting him walk all over humanity while he decided that labeling others as naughty or nice is Santa's divine right.

She feels sick. No, fuck that. She feels *done*.

She realizes that her husband is no longer the jolly man she married who preaches about peace on Earth and the goodness inside all. Santa has turned into the kind of man who calls women *females*. The wonderful Santa Claus is now just another guy belittling others for issues that truely stem from his own insecurities and failures. It may be easier for him to condemn others than to confront the cracks in his own character, but that doesn't mean Gertie has to continue being complicit in his shortcomings.

Santa's cruelty is no longer his problem, now it's hers too. And, thanks to her latest binge of femme fatale fiction, she's ready to unleash a shit ton of feminine rage. Straightening her spine, she lifts her chin proudly. Her heart is pounding with a sense of purpose she hasn't felt in ages. Enough is enough. She's ready to confront her husband, and save their sleigh. It's time for a reckoning.

Mrs. Claus steps into the garage, her boots hitting the ground with force. The sound is loud and abrupt, because she *wants* them to hear her coming. Santa towers over the sleigh with his hands clenched around the handle of the axe. His expression is thunderous, his arms raised as if to lay down the law by bringing down the blade. But before he can strike, Mrs. Claus steps into the light.

"That's enough!"

Santa's jaw drops in surprise, as if he's forgotten that his wife isn't just some side character in his story. "Gertie—" he begins, but she cuts him off with a look so sharp it could cut cookie dough.

"Don't you dare," she snaps, stepping forward with a forceful authority like she's never known. "Don't you dare try to explain your actions to me, Nick. I've let you dismiss me for too long as you've grown more and more obsessed with your precious Naughty List."

Santa rolls his eyes, "This is not the time."

"Oh, don't you roll your eyes at me." Her unflinching gaze bores into her husband so strongly that his shoulders slacken and he drops the axe. "You've crossed a line, Mr. Claus. How about I give you a taste of your own medicine, big boy."

"What I need is for you to stop overreacting, so quit bothering me while I take care of Christmas business and go make me some coffee!" Santa's never yelled at his wife before, but he's already overwhelmed by the devious sleigh, he has no patience for Mrs. Claus.

The room falls deathly silent, not even the wind dares to interject as Gertie unwinds her scarf from her neck. She stares at Santa while slowly folding the fabric neatly, then dropping it to the floor beside her. Mrs. Claus repeats the action with her hat, removing it with an unsettling calm before dropping it on top of the scarf. Santa is nervous, unsure of how his wife is reacting to him blowing up, but knowing that this is the calm before some sort of storm.

Startled by the shift in his wife, Santa searches for the words that will turn her back into the docile female he's grown accustomed to. But she's done letting him run around unchecked, and she's about to show him just what it means to be powerless.

He opens his mouth in hopes that something wise and strong comes out, but the only thing spoken is a silencing, "*Hush,*" by Gertie. The look she gives as she saunters up to him sends a shiver down his spine. It's a look of power, the look of a woman who is no longer willing to tolerate his shit.

"You've been so focused on punishing others," she says with a tone made of steel. "But have you ever thought about what it feels like? To be judged? To be made to feel small?" She tilts her head, her eyes drifting pointedly down to the crotch of his pants before slowly climbing back up to his face.

Santa swallows hard. He's fully dressed, but it's like she has him exposed, stripped and bared down to the ugliest parts. His hands twitch at his sides, but he knows he can't move. Mrs. Claus has him pinned in place, utterly helpless under her scrutiny.

Reaching up to feather a light touch down his fluffy, white beard, she whispers conspiratorially, "Well, I have a secret too." Mrs. Claus locks eyes with him. "While you're out there wasting your time away in your office, I spend my days in the sweltering kitchen. Glistening rivulets of sweat drop down the valley between my breasts, but it's not the ovens that have me hot and bothered." She steps closer, until their bodies are touching just enough to make Santa uneasy. "It's the books. Do you want to know what kind of novels I read when I'm all alone at night, wearing nothing but my apron and some flour?"

Her hand dips to his chest, and she closes her eyes as she feels the frantic beating of his heart against her palm, savoring the sweet harmony of his complete fear. With a wicked smile, she lowers her voice into a husky whisper, "I read smut."

She presses harder into him, pushing him back until he stumbles. Mrs. Claus guides him, not even hiding the fact that she smiles every time he trips over his own laces, until his back hits the cold wooden front of the sleigh.

"My latest reads have all been about strong women who break fragile men. And I've learned a thing or two that I'm eager to share with you. Get in the sleigh," she directs Santa with a nod of her head. There's no room for argument. No space for defiance. Tonight, Santa is completely at Mrs. Claus' mercy. And she's not feeling very forgiving.

# CHAPTER FIVE

"Into the sleigh, Nick," she commands.

Santa hesitates, his eyes flicking towards Sylas before returning to her. Any protest dies on his tongue when her fingers grip his cheeks and pinch together, pouting his lips like a puckerfish. "You don't get to speak. Not until I say so."

She forces his head to nod, pushing and pulling him as he gives in to her control. After she releases him, Santa walks over to the side of the sleigh. The polished wood creaks under his weight as he climbs in, but the way he slinks to his place on the bench makes his large frame suddenly look smaller.

Mrs. Claus follows, swaying her luscious hips confidently. She steps up and gestures for Santa to move. He obeys, offering his hand as she climbs in beside him.

"Now," she says, the authority strong in her voice, "sit right here." Spreading her legs slightly, she pats her thighs with a knowing smile. "You're going to bend over my lap, Santa, like the naughty boy you are."

His face flushes with embarrassment, but one raised eyebrow from her and he shifts into position, lowering his belly across her lap. Sylas steadies himself as Santa adjusts. Mrs. Claus grabs the waistband and tugs his pants down, exposing his bare ass to the cold. A breeze from the open door wafts across Santa's cheeks, pebbling his backside with goosebumps.

"Now tell Madame Claus what you want for Christmas." she taunts, her tone dripping with condescension, turning Santa's own tradition against him.

Santa shifts awkwardly, his pride shrinking with every shuffle to get comfortable. It feels so wrong being bent over like this. Just moments ago, he was towering over his sleigh with an axe, and now he's helpless, his asshole exposed under the bright overhead lights. Before he can gather his thoughts, her hand lands sharply on the fleshiest spot of his backside with a firm swat, the sound echoing through the room.

"Oh, I've got it wrong, haven't I?" Madame Claus mocks. "You're not getting anything for Christmas. It's too bad that little tantrum with the axe earned you a one-way ticket to the Naughty List." Another hard smack follows, landing a blow on top of the already forming hand print, the outline of her palm so clearly defined as it welts. "Now," she says, leaning close enough for the breath of her commanding whisper to tickle his ear, "tell Madame Claus how badly you've been behaving."

Santa bites down a grunt. He's outnumbered by these evil smut readers and has nowhere to go. Reluctantly, he mutters a half-hearted apology for his actions, but the words barely make sense.

Madame Claus shakes her head and delivers another blow, this time harder and on the same raw spot. "Not good enough." she snaps. "Say it. 'I've been a very naughty boy.'"

Santa pushes himself up off her lap, ready to protest. "You're being ridiculous, I'm not saying that."

"That's where you're wrong, Santa baby." Madame Claus presses a firm hand on his back, guiding him until he's forced down into place. "I'm just getting started. If you want to be able to sit down when you deliver toys tomorrow night, you're going to repeat after me. 'I, Santa.'"

His head hangs low, defeat washing over him like a cold shower. Softly, he repeats, "I, Santa."

*Smack.*

"What the hell, Gertie? I said it!" Santa tries to push himself up again, but she holds him down easily. Years of kneading dough have made her strong, and he's no match for her grip.

"You will address me as Madame Claus," she says, punctuating the command with another firm slap. "And when you speak to me, you will annunciate. Do it again."

"I, Santa," he growls, but repeats the words.

"Am a very, *very* naughty boy."

"Am a very naughty boy," he mutters.

Her fingers trail across his skin, manicured ruby nails raking over the fine white hairs on his exposed buns. The redness from her spankings are stark against his pale flesh as a cornucopia of welts rise up. "Do you enjoy being punished?" she croons.

Santa tenses, unsure of how to respond. "What do you want from me, Gerti—Madame Claus?" he corrects himself quickly, his glutes clenching from fear because he almost said the wrong name. "I did what you wanted. I'm admitting that I'm a very naughty boy."

Madame Claus lets out a disdainful chuckle. "I said *very* twice, and you didn't. That sounds like defiance."

Santa huffs in frustration, almost rolling off her lap. "Now, hold on! That's not fair! How was I supposed to know to count your words? You're just setting me up to fail!"

Her laughter is biting and remorseless. "You think it's unfair?" She shakes her head, sending white locks bouncing around as she tsks. "How ironic. You've spent ages judging others, yet you balk when faced with rules you don't agree with. Well, Santa, let me be the one to help you down off your high horse. Or should I say, your patriarchal pony?"

Madame Claus stands abruptly, rolling Santa off her lap with a swift shove. He lands on the floor of the sleigh, momentarily stunned. Before he can gather himself, she plants the sole of her boot on his chest, pressing gently but firmly until he's flat on his back.

Towering above him, she crosses her arms over her ample chest, her entire aura cool and commanding. "Tonight, you're going to do everything I say. Do you understand?"

"Yes, Madame Claus," he replies, the words leaving his lips without hesitation.

She didn't expect him to yield so easily, but as she gazes down at the disheveled man beneath her boot, a thrill of pure power surges to her pussy. Santa's so uncharacteristically vulnerable. Pressing harder, she feels his chest rise and fall beneath her foot, relishing the rhythm of his breath.

"I'm going to make you wish that you never made a Naughty List."

# CHAPTER SIX

A wicked glint shines in her eye as Madame Claus wiggles her nose, casting elven magic over Santa. Silver sparkles swirl around him, glittering in the air before settling on his lap. Propping himself up on his forearms, he stares down as the shimmering dust sinks into the fabric of his sweatpants. Tingles spread over his dick like invisible hands stroking him.

His breath hitches as the warmth quickly turns to something else. The sensation solidifies, and with a faint metallic clink, the glitter transforms. Gleaming bars of precious metals weave together, wrapping delicately around his cock and forming a ring around his balls, creating an intricate chastity cage. Santa's jaw drops with disbelief as the final sparkles disappear leaving him trapped in a new kind of prison.

"What did you do to my dick?" he shouts, frantically tugging his pants down to his knees. His voice trembles with shock. He stares in horror at the delicate, impenetrable web of metal encasing his tender bits, each bar holding him firmly in place.

Madame Claus' smile shines brightly with smug satisfaction as she admires her handiwork. She reaches down and gives the caged cock a firm shake, testing the tightness and durability. Satisfied with how it molds to Santa's body, she releases it with a smirk. "It's a snug fit, but as long as you don't get hard, it shouldn't hurt too badly."

She stands up, stepping over him and straddling his chest. Pulling her skirt up to reveal her thighs, she gives Santa a glimpse of her arousal. The wet spot on her lace trimmed, holly-berry-red silk panties grows with need as she looks down at him. Having her pussy so close sends a jolt of excitement through Santa's body, but the sharp pinch of the cage holds firm.

Madame Claus strokes a finger over the gusset of her panties, her feathered touch slow and deliberate. Santa's eyes are glued to the spot where her fingers tease. She's tantalizing, brushing lightly over the fabric that separates her from her clit.

"That's right, look at me," she hums. "You're such a good boy, watching as I strip away my clothes, and your authority."

Her hands caress her body, dancing along her full curves as she sways her hips, dragging out the moment. Santa wants to look away, to defy her, but he can't. Every move she makes is calculated to keep him tethered to her will. With a sultry turn, she faces away from him. Hiking her sweater up just beneath her bra, her hips continue swaying as if she's performing for an adoring audience, instead of just her husband and his sleigh. She tosses the sweater up over her head and flings it back onto Santa.

Santa barely manages to claw the cable knit bundle from his face in time to see Gertie, no, *Madame* Claus, blow him a teasing kiss. Before he can catch his breath, she shimmies out of her skirt with practiced ease. The heavy winter wool twirls through the air like a lasso as Madame Claus puts on a show, gyrating her hips like she's riding a bull. Her plump ass and thick thighs jiggle as she grinds, the string of her thong swallowing deeper into the depth of her luscious crack while she dances. With a loud cowboy cry, she yeets the skirt, launching it across the garage. It lands with a solid thunk on a nearby toolbox, the tools inside rattling from the weight of the crash.

Watching from beneath the duo, Sylas' essence tingles. *Who needs nine ladies dancing, when Mrs. Claus strips like a pro*, he thinks. Earlier, when Santa spoke of immoral urges that humans have, Sylas didn't understand. But now, watching the Queen of the North in all her glory, it starts to make sense. And it has his wooden core knotting up with things he's never felt before.

"Oh, Sylas," she purrs, turning her attention towards their silent observer. She knows he's been observing them, awkwardly waiting while supporting her and Santa in his carriage. Now, it's time for him to join the fun. "Would you be a dear and lend me your reins?"

Sylas stiffens slightly at the dominating, sultry tone she uses with him, his hardwood tightening under this new command. He's only ever obeyed Santa before, but then again no one else has ever needed the sleigh for a favor. Plus, Mrs. Claus asked so sweetly, there isn't a reason to deny her anything she wishes. Which is why Sylas doesn't hesitate when sliding the leather straps over to her. The supple material falls easily into her waiting hands.

"Of course, Mrs. Claus. Where are we headed?"

Madame Claus smirks, as she kneels over her husband. "Now that's a true good boy, eagerly doing my bidding. You could learn a thing or two from Sylas." Her voice is deceptively sweet but with an edge, like peppermint bark broken into jagged pieces.

The wetness of her panties presses warmly against the firm muscles of Santa's thigh. She wraps the reins around her hands, pulling the leather taut with a sharp *snap* that echoes in the garage. Santa flinches under the crack, the action rubbing his leg up against her horny pussy.

"But, my darling sleigh, we're not going anywhere. In fact, I'm going to keep my naughty boy right here. And I want you to be a part of our little fun." Her lips curl into a smile that's somehow both predatory and playful.

Madame Claus senses the way Santa's body tenses beneath her while she flirts with the sleigh. She lets out a soft moan as she rubs against him, humping Santa's thigh with her covered clit as she mocks his jealousy.

"I wonder..." She leans down, pressing her silk covered tits into his flannel shirt. "Should I let Sylas take your place?"

The suggestion burns through him, igniting an uncomfortable blend of envy and panic. His cock throbs inside its cage, and the cool leather of the reins brush against his skin, sending a shiver up his spine. He winces as she lightly slaps the straps against his chest, aiming for the nipples, but he doesn't pull away. The way he lays prone beneath his wife pleases Madame Claus greatly as she gets ready to have her fun.

"Hands above your head, Santa." she instructs, but her tone is more patient now, as though she's coaxing him deeper into submission.

He crosses his wrists above his head, palms up, resting against the smooth surface of the sleigh's floor. As soon as his wrists touch, Madame Claus loops the reins around them, pulling the leather straps taut. The knots she ties are intricate, but swift, like she's done countless times trussing Santa's favorite roasted hen dinners. She gives the reins one last pull, checking the knots before trailing the end of the straps down his face.

"Gertie, that's enough. You've tied them too tightly."

"What did you just call me?" she asks coldly.

# CHAPTER SEVEN

Santa panics for a moment, realizing too late that he forgot to call her Madame Claus. He tries to explain himself, but before he can get a word out, she shoves the reins into his mouth, pushing the leather deep past his teeth.

"Gertie? Darling, the woman who catered to your inflated ego is gone," she sneers. Madame Claus removes the makeshift gag. He coughs and sputters while catching his breath, spilling drool that trails down his beard in a messy string. She watches the saliva fall, her lips curling in disgust.

"Sugar plum, you've made quite the mess. And of course, I'm the one left to clean it up. How typical." Her contemptuous tone packs centuries of frustration into each word.

Santa swallows hard. He tries to lick the drool away, afraid of what she'll do next, but it's no use. The wetness has already soaked onto the sleigh beneath his head. Madame Claus moves with the fluidity of a dancer, crawling over her submissive

Santa. Her hips sway as she straddles his face, grinding as she finds her position. Gripping the top of his head, she twists her fingers through his hair, holding him in place with a steady, commanding pull. Santa's heart pounds, and though he fights against the reins once more, the binds are unyielding.

"Let's clean you up. Hang on Sylas, this may turn into a rocky ride!" She says as she angles her hips lower. The damp gusset of her panties presses against Santa's beard, dragging across his chin slowly. Her lust overwhelms him, making his mouth water more. She continues to wipe his face, using her thong like a napkin.

Just the other night, Santa's favorite podcast said *only simps eat pussy.* But the longer she rides his face, the harder it becomes to hold out. Not when it's so easy to let his mind quiet, focusing only on the sensation, the pressure, and the heat between them. He suffocates on her sex, her weight pinning him harder into Sylas beneath him. His mustache scratches against her clit, pulling soft hums of satisfaction from her that shoot longing straight to Santa's cock.

The friction causes her panties to shift, exposing one glistening lip and a hint of her copper curls. It's taking everything in Santa to keep himself from tasting her gingerbread cookie. Without thinking, he darts his tongue out and strokes along the faint sliver of pink peeking out from behind the silk. Madame Claus stills, tightening her hold in his hair as she tilts his head back.

"Look at me, you pathetic little man. Did you just taste my cunt without permission?" her voice is icy as she snaps at him.

Santa instinctively shrinks back, as though he could hide from her reprimand, but there's nowhere to go. Her legs cage him in, her arousal intoxicating as she casually slides her panties to the side with her free hand. A single drop of her cunt juices splashes onto his lips. Warm and sticky, the wetness clings to the coarse white beard hairs like tinsel caught on a tree branch.

"If you want this pussy, all you need to do is ask."

His senses are overwhelmed, he's utterly consumed by her scent, her taste, and the gleam of Madame Claus' delicately dripping lady-dew. Santa's throat tightens as he swallows the pooling cum. The tang of her lingers as he grovels beneath her. His voice cracks as he speaks. "Madame Claus, may I please eat your decadent pussy?"

A sharp laugh escapes her. "Stick out your tongue."

He stretches it out obediently, trembling in anticipation. He swears he can feel the pulse of her heartbeat, the blood thrumming through her plump coochie lips. She hovers close, so close that he can feel the heat of her slick without any contact. Santa's mouth waters, aching for her, but Madame Claus only teases him.

"Prove to me you want it. Beg for it." The

space between them is torturous, but she doesn't dip any lower. "Then, I might let that naughty tongue of yours pleasure me."

The power she wields over him makes her hornier, coating Santa in her warm melted butter. He inhales the rawness of her, a mixture of musk and snickerdoodles, the smell so sweet and spicy. He knows she wants it, wants him, but can also tell that her real pleasure comes from watching him suffer beneath her.

His wet muscle remains out, catching every drop of her. Santa swirls her cream around, swishing it like he's tasting a fine wine. He's a man who loves food, and right now his favorite snack is Madame Claus.

"You're exquisite. Like vanilla icing melting over a fresh, hot oatmeal cookie. Even my elves don't make candy as sweet as you. I'm begging you to pour your milky molasses down my throat. Fuck my face with your full bodied flavor."

"Such a filthy mouth, Mr. Claus." She chastises, but her tone is full of satisfaction. "Clean yourself up."

With that, she presses her substantial thighs against his face, granting him access to her Madamehood. Santa groans into her, shaking his head from side to side so his tongue wags against her slit. He revels in the way he's smothered between her legs, licking and sucking greedily. The sleigh beneath them rocks gently, his creaking frame barely masking the sloppy, obscene sounds that fill

HOLLY WILDE

the garage.

# CHAPTER EIGHT

E ven with the side door still open and letting in the frigid air, things are getting hot and steamy inside the garage. A curious tingling creeps across Sylas, the energy coursing through him uncomfortably. It reminds him of the unfamiliar sensations he felt while reading the forbidden book from the Naughty List. The sleigh's sleek, polished body trembles slightly as Madam Claus grips onto his sides, her fingers digging into the smooth cherry paint job as she steadies herself.

His reins, which were meant for guiding him through the skies, now serve a much different purpose. They're keeping Santa pinned under Madame Claus' control. Santa's voice echoes from underneath his wife, calling the space under her tuft of copper hair a cookie. But the thing Santa's nibbling on is nothing like the cookies and milk Sylas is used to having in his carriage. Whatever Santa's eating, it's doing a number on Madame Claus.

"Suck my cunt, you naughty boy." She grits

through her teeth while mashing her muff against Santa's obedient tongue. Madame Claus' body tightens, her movements becoming more insistent as she rides Santa's face. The man is lost in the drenched heat of her thighs, his gasps and groans choking around mouthfuls of her sticky release.

Madame Claus lifts herself just enough to hover above Santa's face, depriving him of her taste once again. Santa's beard is slick, shining with her wetness, and his eyes are filled with desperation.

"That's enough for now." She stands up, looming over the drooling man with a mixture of amusement and satisfaction. "You did a good job, Santa sweetie, making me so wet and horny. But I'm tired of tongue play. I want my pussy stretched."

She gets up and takes a seat on the driver's bench. Tapping the toe of her boot against the cock cage, Madame Claus checks to see if Santa's had any reaction to her. It's obvious he has, the way his bulge pushes against the bars. She doesn't take pity on her submissive Santa, in fact, she decides to enhance his displeasure. Looping her thumbs through the waistband of her panties, she shimmies them off, carefully sliding them over her black leather snow boots. They rest heavily in her palm, soaked through with spit and cum. Madame Claus leans over and places them in Santa's mouth, crotch first, gagging him with the red silk and lace.

"Since you want to act like a little twat online, then you can be treated like one. Pussies need panties, so enjoy choking on mine, Pussy Claus."

She laughs cruely before sitting back again. Madame Claus dips her fingers down and twirls the ginger pubic hair thoughtfully while looking at her bound, gagged, and caged husband. Santa's sausage pushes the limits of his **cage**, his dick struggling for any inch of room it can get. The purpled skin of his attempted penis prison break makes Madame Claus even hornier. But she isn't in the mood to let a misogynistic prick up her chimney tonight.

"Sylas, you look so good beneath Santa, so hard and ready."

Here she is, fingers teasing herself while the most powerful man in the world is at her feet, but all she can do is fantasize about the obedient sleigh supporting them both. "Get on your knees, Santa." She orders, shifting her feet so that it's easier for him to comply. He raises up until he's perfectly positioned at eye level with her wetness. "I was hoping to get fucked by a good man tonight, but since there's none around, I'll settle for a wood man instead."

She leans closer to the speaker, her voice dropping to a sultry whisper only Sylas can hear. "I refuse to fuck my husband until he changes his ways. Sylas, won't you ride your sleighhood over here and take care of me?"

"Madame Claus," he replies softly with a hint of sadness, "I don't have a sleighhood."

Her red nails leave a teasing trail down his smooth panelboard as she asks, "Would you like one?"

"Yes, please!" Sylas' voice blares through the speaker, startling Santa, who winces at the sound. Madame Claus smirks, amused by both of their reactions. She's looking forward to putting Santa in his place by putting Sylas up her snatch. With a sinister wink of her eye and a subtle twitch of her nose, she begins to weave her magic.

It starts as a warm hum beneath her cum slicked fingertips, her nails glowing a bright crimson as she traces an invisible cylinder in the air between her thighs where she's sitting on the bench. The heat of her power swirls like molten energy, calling to the wood and metal of the sleigh. Wisps of silver and red light spiral upward, twisting together. The glowing streams coil tighter and tighter as they take form.

A sleek rod emerges from the seat, the base of it rooted firmly in place. It rises to an impressive fourteen inches tall, the gleaming chrome vibrating faintly with anticipation. Madame Claus admires her creation, a stick shift of pure pleasure, designed to drive her wild. A dick-shift, if you will. The shaft is thick, smooth, and powerfully sensual. At the top is a rounded, pulsing knob, throbbing with a steady rhythm as if the magic itself is eager to be touched. It hums louder as her fingers curl around the peppermint-striped pole.

Over the centuries, the world around Sylas has been an ever changing landscape, while he's remained the same as the day he was created. That all ends tonight. Gifted with a new appendage, his entire being thrums with excitement as his stiffness stands tall.

Sylas moans through the speaker as she strokes the new sleighhood. His pleasure fills the air, ringing through the room as he cries out. Positioned perfectly at Santa's eye level, the thickness of Sylas' tobogganhood blocks his view of Madame Claus' wet, needy sex. It stirs a deep, shameful embarrassment in Santa, the way his pecker tries to swell from this carnal display. His broad shoulders slump as he lowers his head, trying to avoid watching the pornographic thrill of his wife and his sleigh hooking up.

"Eyes on me," Madame Claus demands. Santa hesitates, but slowly raises his gaze, catching a glimpse of her fierce, unrelenting smile. Her hand moves slowly up and down the shaft, stroking it with teasing, deliberate pumps. The whir of Sylas' intimate appendage grows more frantic as Madame Claus picks up the pace.

Santa's face flushes with humiliation as Madame Claus leans back, spreading her thighs apart to give him the barest hint of what lies behind the peppermint rod, revealing just enough to make his mouth water and his groin ache.

"Look closely." she says as she works the magical wand with expert hands. "This is what satisfaction looks like."

With a twist of her wrist, Madame Claus angles the vibrating dickshift against her slit. A shiver runs through her body as the buzzing sensation teases her folds. She scoots her ass closer, angling her hips until her new toy is perfectly aligned. Propping her boots on Santa's line-backer shoulders, she uses his body for leverage as she adjusts into a position that feels just right.

Madame Claus fully embraces the orgasm that's steadily building between her thighs. She rocks her hips back and forth, the length of the rod parting her wetness as she mocks her husband. "Looks like you're nothing more than a pedestal for me now, oh how the mighty have fallen."

The weight of her boots press down on Santa, forcing him to stay anchored, face to face with the juicy cunt he's been denied. His eyes dart between the toy and her body, powerless to look away as his worst fear comes true. Santa Cuck is in town, but he isn't the one who's coming tonight.

# CHAPTER NINE

S ylas knows this is a game, a twisted dance of power between husband and wife, and that he's merely a tool being used to punish Santa. But right now, he doesn't care. It's intoxicating the way Madame Claus' body responds to him. All he can focus on is the waves of pleasure coursing through his frame as he vibrates harder and faster. He can sense Santa's heavy and uneven breath, thick and panting with titillation, mingling with the wetness of Madame Claus' folds as she works herself against the magic cock. Santa's frustrated groans are dampened by the red panties stuffed in his mouth.

Madame Claus is thriving, having awakened her inner main character energy. She masturbates with her sleigh's package unapologetically while her husband squirms under her boots. Rocking and arching, losing all sense of rhythm, Madame Claus flails on the sleigh's dick as she chases her orgasm. Her body tightens, panting and sweaty, as she gets closer to her climax.

"Tongue my pussy," she commands, yanking the gag from Santa and shoving his face between her thighs.

There's no way Santa can reach her clit from where she holds him, but he knows better than to resist. Her grip is too solid, her body consumed with the promise of release. He begins to lap at the soft, swollen folds, even as they grind against Sylas' vibrating shaft. The salty taste of both cock and cunt fills his mouth at once, and soon, he's greedily licking whatever he can.

Madame Claus' head tilts back, her breath ragged as she rides the edge of pleasure. Her words pour out in gasps, "Suck my juicy cunt you naughty boy! Lick that dick like you know your place!"

The pressure builds, coiling tighter and tighter until she can no longer hold back. Madam Claus is screaming into the night, grinding and crying out with an urgency her captive audience has never seen before. Her climax hits like a blast, her body shaking as the orgasm shatters through her. She trembles uncontrollably, her hands still gripping Santa's hair as she rides out every wave of her pleasure.

Santa still obediently laps at her, his tongue catching the lingering wetness. Madame Claus, still breathless and trembling from the intensity, rises up. She adjusts herself so that she's on her knees, hovering over the cock, her pussy drooling on it hungrily like a slobbery dog over a bone. With a firm grip on Sylas' striped, twitching shaft, she guides the tip to her entrance. Her gaze flicks down to Santa, who remains beneath her, forced to witness every move she makes.

Slowly, deliberately, she begins to sink the rod into her, enveloping it inch by delicious inch with her soaking yuletide yammy. A soft moan crackles through the speakers as the thick shaft parts her, stretching and filling her completely. Lowering her hips only to lift them again, she drags out each thrust as Santa watches, wide-eyed and lips still tingling from the taste of her.

Madame Claus rolls her hips, taking Sylas deeper. She finds that steady rhythm that sends bliss through her core. Glancing over at her husband, bound and staring intently, she notices that his eyes begin flicking between her body and the floor.

She teases. "Do you like watching me take this cock?"

Santa's face tightens, his irritation evident. His balls ache with unspent desire, his dick straining against the confines of its cage. He knows better than to push her, but he can't help himself. "No," he growls, his voice thick with frustration. "I want you to take *my* cock. Not this little toy."

Madame Claus only smirks, not faltering her rhythm as Santa presses on, clearly agitated. "He's just a sleigh, Gertie. Not a real man. Nothing he does can satisfy you. So go ahead, bounce on your inanimate knob and pretend it's everything you want while you really wish you were with a good guy like me who deserves it."

With a sharp slam of her hips, Madame Claus drives herself down, the full length of the chrome disappearing between her thighs until her skin meets the soft cushion beneath her. She doesn't cower while meeting Santa's glare head-on. "Haven't you learned anything yet?" she asks, her voice steady and full of confident authority. "Or do you just want more punishment? I'm not your darling Gertie anymore, you will address me as Madame Claus."

Santa's sneer deepens, but there's a flash of desperation in his eyes as he's forced to remain beneath her while they argue. "Yeah, sure. Whatever you say *Madame* Claus," he spits. "You act like this is the night of your life, but Sylas isn't even fucking you, you do realize that, right? He's just sitting there, being a stupid sleigh. I, however, am a real man with a real cock."

Madame Claus moves her hips in a figure eight as she slides up and down Sylas' North Pole. "I can promise you, I'm not missing anything."

Santa mutters under his breath, his words dripping with disdain. "You're going to regret this when you've had your fun, because while you try to make it up to me, I'll be off delivering gifts to people who actually matter."

"What was that, dear?" Madame Claus keeps smiling, condescending her husband with a hand cupped by her ear as though she were trying to truly hear his grumbling over her moans.

"I said, even if you cuddle up with the sleigh,

you aren't going to feel satisfied. Your empowered feminist act is bullshit, because your female parts only want you to make babies and tend to your husband. You'll never be satisfied with a silly sentient sleigh. So stop playin' and untie me."

She slows, her hips coming to a halt as the toy moves against her g-spot. The vibration against her core is bringing more than just ecstasy, it's giving her clarity. All this time, she's been coddling a man who's never wanted a partner. She was a wife to a guy who really wanted a mommy. Santa doesn't really love her, he just wants someone to cater to his needs without asking for anything in return.

With the snap of her fingers, the vibrating stops. The room falls into an almost eerie silence. Santa's lips twitch into a smug smile, thinking he's won. That he's managed to put her back in her place. But he's wrong, so very wrong.

Madame Claus stands, the slick chrome rod pulling from her wintery wonderland with a loud pop. She looks down at Santa, bound and helpless on the sleigh floor in front of her, with a mix of pity and power. The scent of her spiced gingerbread sex lingers in the air, warm and sweet, but her tone is anything but.

"You're all too right," she purrs, running a finger down the slope of his nose. "Sylas isn't a man by your standards, but neither are you." She presses her palm dramatically against her forehead as she rolls her eyes. "Silly me, thinking you could ever be my happily ever after. I thought I felt love, but it turns out I was just following that old biological pull to nurture someone and share my life with them."

She drops her hand and narrows her eyes as she stares down Santa. His jaw clenches beneath his snowy beard, and he refuses to look away, but Madame Claus doesn't stop. She leans in close, her tits pushed into his face, thanks to the pushup bra she's still wearing. "As far as Sylas being a man goes, well, things can always change around here."

Without warning, she roughly grabs Santa's bound hands and brings him down from the sleigh. Falling off the platform and onto the cement floor with a thud, Santa groans in protest. Pulling him a few feet clear of Sylas, she leaves him behind, turning her attention back to the sleigh.

Raising her hand in the air, she wiggles her nose and chants a few lilting words in an old language Santa hasn't heard in centuries. The air around the sleigh shimmers with light. The wooden planks creak and groan as it starts to warp. Levitating off the ground, a shape takes form, the metal runners bending and folding into human legs. The sloping front solidifies into a broad, muscular body. Sylas' belly, the roundness, not unlike Santa's, rises and falls with each breath.

His face, sculpted with a strong jawline covered in neatly trimmed white scruff, and soft rosy cheeks, gives Sylas a rugged yet approachable beauty. His nose is straight and defined, with faint freckles adding to his sweet charm. His full lips stretch into a boyish grin as he gazes over to

Madame Claus, raking over her full figure with his stunning green eyes.

As the magic moves lower, Madame Claus grins mischievously. His pubic hair curls into delicate clusters of mistletoe, the tiny white berries nestled within framing his strong, hard cock. Below, his jingle bell balls rattle to life, filling the room, and Madame Claus' cunt, with Christmas cheer. She hums approvingly at the magical fourteen incher that she crafted earlier still hanging between Sylas' legs. Obviously, she wanted to keep the best part of him.

"Well, won't you look at that. You were absolutely right, Nick. I do need a man. I just don't need you."

Santa scoffs, struggling against the ropes binding his wrists. "Nonsense. You think you can build a guy the way we build toys in my workshop?"

Laughing, Madame Claus gestures toward Sylas as she saunters over to the naked man staring down in awe at his new body. His balls jingle joyfully as she fists his shiny rod. Pulling him forward towards Santa, she leads Sylas like a reindeer, her grip around his stocking stuffer firm yet comfortable. He moves effortlessly under her control, figuring out how to walk on legs with measured steps until he's standing over Santa.

"I want you to take a good, very long look, and tell me, dear, did I build a toy? Or did I build a man? Because what I see is someone bigger than you'll ever be, both in spirit and...well, I'm sure you can see it, too." She says, eyeing Santa's caged purple Christmashood.

Santa's eyes drift towards the floor in defeat. He knows he's been beaten and belittled, but begrudgingly, there's nothing he can do about it. Nevertheless, he persists. "Fuck you both," Santa groans, the arrogance still high and mighty in his voice.

"Fuck us both? As you wish."

# CHAPTER TEN

"Excuse me?" Santa blurts out as his eyes snap to the two towering over him.

"Oh, you heard me right, dear. You made a Christmas wish, and this time of year things like that tend to come true."

"That's not what I meant you incorrigible cunt," his voice filled with alarm.

A knot tightens in Santa's stomach as his eyes track the tip of Sylas' cock, noticing how it's frosted with white anticipation. The subtle scent of peppermint fills his nostrils as Madame Claus brings Santa's head closer to the red and chrome rod. She wipes her thumb across Sylas' shining head, gathering the precum like it's buttercream. It glistens as she brings it to her lips, tasting it leisurely while intensely scrutinizing Santa.

"Mmm, so good. Try it."

Santa's heart pounds in his chest as she swipes more of the sickly sweet goodness, pressing the warm, slick cum onto his pursed lips. "Open up the hangar for the sleighhood to land in." She's playful but authoritative, pushing her fingers past his teeth. Pressing in and out, she makes Santa suck on her fingers until he swallows Sylas's minty man juice.

"That's it. Sylas is gonna give you a white Christmas, but first you gotta practice before you step under the mistletoe. We wouldn't want you to embarrass yourself as you kiss what's underneath those vibrant green leaves of his."

She continues pumping her two fingers in a steady, unrelenting rhythm, teasing him with her nails. Santa's mouth betrays him, parting involuntarily, lips pursing around her protrusion as if by instinct. A sultry smile brightens her face as Madame Claus preps Santa for giving head. Her thumb traces his lower lip, coaxing him further into submission.

His tongue hangs thick and heavy in his talk box, the taste of peppermint cum flooding his senses. It's an odd mixture, cool like toothpaste, but with a sticky sweetness that clings to his taste buds like fudge. The sensation isn't entirely unpleasant, though Santa doesn't want to admit how much he likes this.

"There we go," she coos softly, withdrawing her fingers with deliberate slowness, a trail of saliva stretching between them before it snaps. She wipes the residue off her fingers and onto Sylas' cock with a languid motion. She tugs her new man over, propping the peppermint pole in front of Santa's face. "You know the rules," she purrs while tilting her husband's head until his eyes are in line with the dickhole. "Under the mistletoe, you kiss what's in front of you."

Her fingers tighten in his hair, the slight tug sending a jolt down his spine as she brings his head towards Sylas. The soft brush of Sylas' tip against Santa's lips feels surprisingly hot, like making out with a mug of hot chocolate instead of a metal thing. Madame Claus presses them together more firmly, urging Santa to go deeper. His hesitant tongue slides across the head, licking the bead of precum. A shudder that he can't suppress ripples through Sylas beneath the delicate pressure of Santa's lips.

Madame Claus surprises them both by dropping to her knees and taking a place beside Santa. "Let me show you how it's done. We'll start with the basics. Mr. Claus, you may now kiss your wife."

She leans in, her lips brushing his with a soft familiar touch, like she's done a million times before. His instinct is to pull back, startled by a softer side of Madame Claus shining through. However, though she kneels beside him, Santa is aware that this isn't an act of submission from her.

Madame Claus is no longer the adoring wife, Gertie, anymore. She's transformed into a strict teacher, and now Santa finds himself the unwilling student. She's leading, and he's learning, forced to comply with her every instruction. Madame Claus flirts with her tongue, deepening the kiss. It's passionate and loving, and if Santa didn't have his hands bound by the wrists and his cock in a cage, he would consider this moment romantic.

She murmurs words against his lips that he can't understand, but he doesn't care because it feels like he got his wife back. She rakes her hands through his hair, pulling him closer to her, drawing their love deeper. He's so enamored with the kiss that he doesn't realize until the bulge presses into his cheek that his wife wasn't pulling him into her, Madame Claus was positioning them closer to Sylas.

Her hands twist a little harder at the top of Santa's head, making sure he doesn't pull back. "Now, kiss me again."

She poises the head between them, then loops her tongue out under the tip. Dancing it back and forth on the underside of the dick, she begins to make out with Santa while they simultaneously suck on Sylas. It's hard to tell where Santa ends and Madame Claus begins, everything is just warm, wet and thrilling. Sylas' erection twitches between them, drizzling his syrupy precum in their mouths like he's topping waffles.

Madame Claus' breath fogs the chrome shaft as she whispers, "Don't stop." They teasingly brush against each other as they lick lower. She guides Santa along the cock, controlling each hesitant moment. Santa can feel tension coiling under the metallic finish, the shaft thickening between them.

At the base, Madame Claus pops one of the jingle balls into her mouth with a smug smirk, her eyes never leaving Santa's. With a playful shove, she instructs him to do the same. The jingle rings through his head as he rolls his tongue over the noisy orb.

Pulling back with a soft thwack, she tells him, "Show me what you've learned."

Her gaze is sharp and evaluating as she waits for Santa to obey. He does, kissing his way back to the tip, leaving behind a wet and sloppy trail.

"You've led the sleigh for years, don't you think it's time someone drives into you?"

# CHAPTER ELEVEN

Sylas is used to staring at ass, but not like how he is tonight. Perceiving reindeer in front of him when he was a sleigh is completely different than using eyes to check out Madame Claus' gorgeous, voluptuous booty as she bends down to untie Santa. He doesn't even hear her command his old boss to get down on his hands and knees, Sylas is too busy navigating all the sensory input being a human comes with. The lights glare differently, his skin is cold but also sweaty and hot at the same time, and his cock is pulsing so much that it's almost painful.

While he was a sleigh, he never knew real pain, but then again, he never knew pleasure like this before either. It isn't just his rod that responds to touch. It's everywhere he has skin. While Madame Claus and Santa were on their knees kissing him,

Sylas found his hands instinctively roving his body. He loved tweaking and pinching his nipple most of all, the little stings enhancing the warmth peppering his dick with affection.

Madame Claus steadies Sylas' hands on Santa's head before standing up. The look in her eyes tells him that she's transferring the reins to him, metaphorically. She doesn't utter a word, but she doesn't have to. Sylas is trained on trying out new maneuvers and learning new tricks. Right now, he gets to drive.

Stepping behind Sylas, Madame Claus presses her hips against his, guiding his movements, showing him how to thrust with control. In and out, they move his rod back and forth. Santa sputters, drooling as he struggles to take it. Sylas's butt gets sticky, and for a moment he wonders if humans leak from back there as well. When Madame Claus starts to rub her hairy mound against him, making him wetter as she humps, he realizes it's her that's making the mess.

Their rhythm is steady and slow, giving Santa plenty of time to breathe between thrusts. The slick slapping of Santa's throat as he sucks, the jingling of Sylas' ballsack, and moans from all three of them turn the garage into a hedonistic Christmas carol.

Madame Claus releases Sylas once his cock takes over the pace, the throbbing rod demanding that he fuck harder and faster. She watches her husband's mouth get plugged and starts imagining how festive he'd look with his ass filled too. It turns her on fantasizing about what naughty ways she can use his body. The moisture between her thighs demands attention, and she knows just how to claim her next orgasm. Smoothing her hand with her pussy fluids, she saunters behind Mr. Claus and wipes her cum down his backside.

"Looks like you're swapping out the Christmas Team for being double-teamed tonight!"

Madame Claus conjures a swirl of green and gold magic that gathers in her palm. It twists and shapes, spiraling until it forms a small, perfectly sculpted silicone Christmas tree. Its conical form tapers to a rounded point at the top, and flares at the base to ensure that the toy is safe for anal play. The plug's smooth surface glistens with emerald green glitter that catches the light. As she turns the plug in her hand, something inside it jingles playfully. The soft, cheerful chime mirrors the steady pounding of Sylas' jingle balls as Santa's face get's thoroughly fucked by the sleigh.

Santa's gasps are shallow, but it's hard to tell if it's because he's sucking cock, or because he's nervous about having something shoved up his ass. Madame Claus reaches up to Santa's face and instructs him to spit in her palm. A waterfall of saliva falls from his mouth, which she uses to grease his tight hole.

"Get ready, because tonight you're taking packages in the back door instead of the chimney!"

Santa stiffens, Sylas' tip slamming against his tonsils, as Madame Claus presses the smooth toy against his skin. His cheeks clench like he doesn't want to sit on top of the tree, but since he's the star of the season, he has no choice.

"You're going to want to relax. This is going in, no matter what, so you decide how easy you want it to be." With a steady push and some gentle wiggling, she plugs the Christmas tree into Santa's ass. The coolness of the toy contrasts with the heat of his body, making him pucker his asshole defensively. But the magic that molded this plug helps it sink in, the design adjusting to his body perfectly as it stretches him just enough to loosen him for later.

Santa gasps, sending the tiny bells inside the plug into action, rolling them around like they're applauding how tight he is. The smooth surface glides to a stop as the wide base settles snugly against him. He keeps moaning around the cock, the vibration of it making Sylas feel like he's engaging in overdrive with how hard he pounds Santa's mouth. Sylas feels something deep within his jingle balls. They rattle and clang, ringing out as they tighten. He doesn't know what's about to happen, but right now it feels good. He doesn't think he could stop even if he tried.

Like icing bursting from a piping bag that has too many bubbles, something white and thick sprays from Sylas' dick hole. He pumps his cream into Santa's open maw, the man staring up at Sylas in surprise as his tongue is coated in cum. Sylas watches in awe, half wanting to close his eyes and savor the moment, half unable to look away from his first sexual encounter.

As well written as that smut book was, it couldn't have conveyed just how good an orgasm really feels. There just aren't the words to describe the way his body tingled, and also got hot, while waves of what felt like electrically charged water moved through him. Up his legs, through his stomach, causing his heart to hammer, making his arms feel weak, though simultaneously making him feel so strong. Being human is complex, but being a man with your cock in the mouth of another is really beautiful.

"Don't swallow," Madame Claus orders Santa, moving back up to the space beside Sylas. "You're gonna hold that cum until he's spilled every last drop. Nod if you understand."

Santa bobs his head enthusiastically, the corners of his mustache glistening as he splashes a little of the sweetness onto his beard. He takes it like a champ, cheeks puffed out like a bowl brimming with decadent penis soup. Santa's careful to spill as little as possible while collecting Sylas' Christmas essence, unsure of the punishments that would follow if he were to leak some cumdrops.

Once Sylas has finished, Madame Claus moves him aside with a firm but gentle push. "Now, be a dear and fetch everyone's clothes. I need to lie down." She instructs. Sylas scurries off, gathering the discarded garments to create a makeshift bed. He pauses after draping Madame Claus' pile onto the floor, realizing that Santa is still wearing his button up flannel and has sweatpants around his ankles. Figuring out how to do buttons is hard for the former sleigh, his fingers refusing to fit the tiny disks through the holes without fumbling. Once he gets the last button unfastened, he peels back the fabric that's clung to Santa throughout their sexual escapade.

Tugging off Santa's boots and pants proves to be more difficult. Sylas uses the bells shoved up Santa's ass as a guide. If they jingle, then he knows he's moving the man too much while stripping him, risking having Santa spit out the mouthful he's still holding. No ringing is the goal, and somehow Sylas manages to get the job done. He's feeling confident in his skills, getting more and more used to maneuvering his new body.

Sylas lays out the remaining clothes, crafting a cozy, albeit lumpy, love nest of winter wear. He takes Madame Claus' hand and helps her down to their bed. Santa stays obediently on all fours while they get comfortable, his neck cramping from holding the awkward position of having an open, cum filled mouth.

Madame Claus lays back and splays her legs open. Angling her sex towards Santa, her pussy gets wetter as she commands, "Crawl to me, and when you get here, spill all of that icing on my cookie. I want you to frost my cunt with Sylas' cum."

Propping herself up on her forearms, Madame Claus watches Santa crawl towards her.

The anticipation builds as he slowly inches closer, cautiously making his way over to her. With a tilt of his head, he spills the mouthful onto her eager clam, the sticky sweetness cascading over her skin like molten sugar.

The rich essence mingles with her warmth, transforming her sex into a tantalizing sight, like cinnamon rolls buried under thick, creamy icing. Each indulgent strand of liquid sweetness glistens as it drops, igniting a rush through her body.

"Eat it," she commands.

# CHAPTER TWELVE

Santa stares down at the sticky mess between his wife's thighs, watching as the thick, white sleigh-seed trickles slowly down her crack, leaving a glistening trail in its wake. He's surprised by the sheer volume of jolly joy juice Sylas has released. Santa's never sucked off a guy before, but even if he had, he wouldn't have imagined anyone could unleash this much. Sylas' load is spilled forth like he'd been saving up over the centuries. But Santa doesn't get to ponder the anatomical logistics of objects-turned-human, because there's a Christmas feast nestled between Madame Claus' thighs, and he's been ordered to devour every last drop.

He leans in, his tongue darting tentatively, scooping up a glob of the hot, syrupy mixture. Madame Claus lets out a pleased sigh as Santa continues to lap slowly, savoring the fragrant peppermint and gingerbread cream. Her fingers tangle in his hair to guide him deeper. It's a fitting justice, keeping Santa buried in her bush. Keeping Santa on his hands and knees is sparing those innocent souls he's been judging so harshly for reading books they love.

If only the world could see him now—Santa Claus, the figurehead of righteousness, dutifully swallowing another man's cum from his own wife's tender cunt. Madame Claus believes that this moment should be enough to strip Santa of his moral authority, but just in case he still hasn't dismantled his internalized toxic masculinity, she has one more trick up her sleeve. And it's getting Sylas' dick up Santa's ass.

The beauty of a metal penis is its unwavering hardness. Sylas stands beside the Claus couple, entranced by what just happened. A torrent of frosting spilled from his tip, and the sight of it in Santa's mouth ignited a curious desire within Sylas. He wonders what it tastes like. Sylas casts a subtle, pleading look at Madame Claus, silently seeking permission to squeeze his cock. With a gracious nod, she gives her approval, and Sylas eagerly wraps his hand around his sturdy shaft.

As streams of dew begin to trickle from his tip, Sylas can't resist sampling his own essence. The bright cool burst surprises him, like eating a crisp winter morning. Swiping another drop, he rolls it between his fingers, marveling at how smooth it is despite being slightly thick.

"It seems like you're ready to jingle those balls once more, Sylas. Are you going to stuff Santa's ass tonight? I'm quite certain that the Christmas tree up there is primed for you to deliver your package." Madame Claus lets out a full belly laugh, pleased with herself for having a jolly fucking night.

The jiggle from her laughter makes it harder for Santa to do his task, as she writhes underneath him. Sylas is captivated by how her tits bounce, and reaches over to feel if they're as plush as they look.

They're even better, soft and squishy like marshmallows bobbing in a cup of hot cocoa. Her nipples, rosy and inviting, decorate her body like ornaments. They pebble into pointed peaks as he pinches gently.

"That's enough, Sylas. It's time to unplug the tree for the night. Replace that toy with your hard cock."

He's sad to let her go, but eager to get his dick wet again. Dashing over, Sylas fixates on Santa's ass. The sight of Santa's heavy balls, painted in the hues of a stunning sunset, contrast beautifully with the gilded cage that keeps his boner compressed. Pinks, blues, and purples tint his veiny, wrinkled skin. Sylas can't resist the urge to soar into that vibrant sky, unable to fight his sleigh instincts.

He dives down, pressing Santa's ballsack against his face. As Sylas drags them along the contours of his own features, he realizes he has no clue what he looks like. He hasn't seen a mirror yet, and was too busy touching himself to discover the characteristics of his face. With imagination, and help from Santa's sack, Sylas explores himself in a new way. Tracing the heavy bags across his forehead, down his nose, he presses the orbs of Santa's sack against his eyelids.

They roll down his face like snowballs tumbling down a hill, until they reach his mouth. Santa melts with a low moan, the sound reverberating against Madame Claus' pussy.

"Stop that, Sylas. You're going to make the man cum, and Santa doesn't deserve it. Only good folks get goodies, isn't that right, Naughty Claus?"

Sylas pulls himself out from his reverie, planting one last kiss, this time on the crushed head of Santa's cock. A pearl of cum drips down, tasting entirely different from his own. While Sylas makes peppermint frosting, Santa's cum is thicker and more velvety, with rich notes of nutmeg and vanilla. Yet there's a fiery edge to Santa's seed that cuts through the sweetness, like eggnog spiked with a heavy pour of alcohol. Sylas guesses that if he were to swallow it down, it would leave a gentle burn behind in his chest, like a spiced holiday hug. But that's not something Sylas will get to experience tonight, or anytime soon, it seems. Madame Claus doesn't appear ready to release Santa from his opulent cage anytime in the near future.

A cheerful jingle above his head reminds Sylas of his latest Christmas mission. It may not be his turn to deliver gifts around the world, but he has a special package to present. As a sleigh, Sylas spent years learning how to delicately land on rooftops, until he excelled at his technique. Now, as a human, he only has mere seconds to become proficient in the art of a soft touch. Otherwise, he might rip out the plug like he's pull-starting a chainsaw. Carefully, Sylas grips the base of Santa's toy, his fingers curling around the silicone. He applies slow, gentle pressure, easing it out with measured tugs.

At first, there's resistance; the band of skin clings tightly, reluctant to release what it's been holding in. Sylas works with the tension, massaging the skin with his free hand, coaxing it to yield. The widest part finally breaks free, unleashing a warm, lingering burn that Santa has to breathe through. With a soft plop, Sylas draws the tip from the slightly pulsing hole. The subtle tremble of Santa's blushing band beckons to Sylas' yule log, pleading to be stretched once more.

He recalls Madame Claus' promise to make Santa's wish come true, and a swell of pride blooms through his entire being. In his past life as a sleigh, he followed many of Santa's commands, but never had his friend made a wish to him. Now, armed with the power of his vibrating cock, he prepares to fulfill Santa's desire, ready to take the jolly man's ass just as he had asked.

The only problem is, Santa's hole is dry. Sylas didn't face this issue with Santa's mouth or Madame Claus' cookie. Why, he wonders, doesn't Santa's hole come with the same natural lubrication? Glancing around and then down at his own body, he searches for anything that might help moisten Santa's entrance. A brief, unsettling thought flickers through his mind—what if he can't make Santa's dreams come true? Sylas lets out an exasperated grunt, the noise releasing frustration, but also sparking an idea.

Sylas realizes that he has a mouth, and those things are wet. All he needs is something to get his watering. He knows just what to do. Reaching between Santa's legs, Sylas rubs along the caged shaft, collecting a healthy coat of Santa's eggnog goodness. Licking the hearty fluid from his hand, he savors its strong, earthy flavor. Swishing around his cheeks, he rolls his tongue around until he's gathered all the saliva he needs.

Leaning over Santa's puckered hole, he lets a strand of spit trail down with practiced precision, hitting the exact spot he's targeting. A smirk tugs at his lips as he admires his own aim. With a steady hand, he lines up the tip, swirling it over the slickend spot until it's coated enough to slide in. The taut skin yields easily, having spent its last resistance on the plug that primed it earlier. Santa's muffled grunts turn to strangled gasps as Madame Claus pushes his face into her pussy, silencing each complaint. Despite the spit, Santa's ass resists him. With a frustrated groan, Sylas pulls out, the separation punctuated with a sloppy pop. His stroking is feverish, matching the pace with which his thoughts swirl. He's so horny, there has to be another way to get wetness out of him.

A bead of release drips onto Sylas' pumping hand, sparking a sudden idea. If Sylas is perpetually hard, then perhaps he has an unlimited supply of cum. And cum is very wet. He jerks his metal cock with the fury of a Black Friday rush. Prodding at the anal opening, he circles it firmly, massaging just enough moisture for him to slip his thumb in. Sylas finger-fucks Santa's ass, pushing knuckle-deep in time with his masturbation. Around them, the world fades into a blur of heat and intensity as they revel in each other's bodies and the primal thrill of being alive.

Sylas finds his hips bucking instinctively into his hand, each thrust bringing him closer to the edge. The release builds, rising from the depths of his jingle balls and surging through his rigid length. He hopes the terrain inside his cock is favorable for such a journey, knowing far too well what it's like taking off to somewhere you don't know. Such is the life of a sleigh, and it's probably the same for a sperm.

The thrill has him counting down like he would before takeoff. "I'm gonna come—oh, five... it's building... four... yes, that's it, Santa... three... two... oh, fuck it's here... one—Ugnhn."

With a final tilt of his hips, Sylas presses the head into Santa's crack. The cum flows like an unending champagne fountain, each hot spurt marking his path. Even as he's spilling over, he thrusts forward, letting his own arousal pave the way as he plunges deeper. With a final tilt of his hips, he wedges the tip into Santa's crack.

"Your ass is so much better than your mouth, Santa." Sylas groans as he slides in and out.

"That's because the shit that comes from there is cleaner than the shit he spouts from his lips." Madame Claus laughs.

Santa's body is too overwhelmed to form words. His tongue feels numb from cleaning up the mess he made on Madame Claus' pussy, his ass is stretched to its limit by a fourteen inch pole, and his cock, still painfully hard, strains against the metal enclosure. Somewhere in the haze of his punishment, though, he begins to understand the lesson Madame Claus is teaching him. It doesn't feel good receiving discipline for rules that are always changing, making it hard for him to know how to behave. Santa may be getting plowed, but there are other seeds being planted tonight too. The seeds of change are nesting in Santa's mind. Questions he's long buried begin to surface, whispering doubts about the rules he's so firmly enforced. Wondering if maybe he did get a tad power-hungry.

He remembers creating the Naughty List himself, as a way to keep busy through the lonely, dark days at the North Pole. Back then, it seemed like a brilliant way to pass the time, a purposeful balance of rewards and consequences. But as the years went by, he became harsher, finding more satisfaction in withholding gifts more than in giving them.

A rush of surrender overtakes him, and for the first time ever, Santa begins to question whether smut is truly as problematic as he once believed. After what Santa's experienced tonight, he sees the truth. He's been so wrapped up in his own self-hatred, his own insecurities, that seeing flaws in others had only amplified his own. Each naughty thing he punishes is just a reflection of what he buries within himself. But when he's drinking up cum and stretching around a toy, Santa doesn't have to worry about any of that. There's no need to think, no need to judge. Just the warm, blissful abandon of letting go.

But then, a sound cuts through the night. A soft, familiar chime, and it's not from anyone's balls or anal toys. The bells echo through the night air, chiming twelve times for midnight. It's officially Christmas Eve.

# CHAPTER THIRTEEN

Santa jolts upright as he realizes that, in mere hours, he's expected to be in the sky, delivering gifts to the first time zone. All of the self-reflection and humility drain from him, his thoughts now overtaken by agitation. Pointing a finger at his wife, he starts releasing his fury.

"How dare you…" he growls before whipping his head to the side. "Sylas, stop fucking me while I'm talking!"

Sylas stills, taken aback by the sudden shift in the evening. Madame Claus narrows her gaze, staring at Santa with icy calm as he turns back to her.

"Do you even realize who I am?" he sneers. "I'm *The* Santa Claus. I'm a motherfucking icon. And who are you? Just my wife, an extension of *me*. Mrs. Santa Claus. Nobody even knows your first name.

And you, Sylas, you're even less important. There are songs written about the reindeer, naming them all off one by one, but you're just a tool. Y'all are no-name bitches, thinking you're important. You really think you could ever matter more than me?"

He waves a dismissive hand at Madame Claus and continues his rant, "See, this is what smut does. It fills your head with delusions. Now, stop being overdramatic, uncage me and go get my breakfast started. I've got a big day ahead."

As he finishes his tirade, he stands, and with a smug grin, thrusts his cock into his wife's face with arrogant satisfaction. The intricate filigree gleams around the almost inhumanly squished dick. His mouth is still wet, and his words land in splatters as he scoffs down at her. "And while you're at it, turn that monster back into a sleigh. Take away his sentience, too. I don't want a repeat of tonight, got it, Gertie?"

Horror-stricken, a tear slips down Sylas' cheek as he realizes that the man he had served and trusted for centuries views him as nothing more than a gadget, disposable and insignificant. His whole sense of being feels like it's deflating, the body he'd only just begun to love slipping away from him before he got a chance to experience it fully. But even worse than losing a form is losing a soul, he can't fathom what that will mean. He closes his eyes, bracing for the impending void, waiting for the magic to snuff him out.

But nothing happens.

Slowly, he peeks to find Madame Claus still laying on the floor, legs spread wide and proud, her gaze unwavering. There's no fear and no hesitation in her eyes, only a feminine ferocity.

"I thought I told you how to address me," she says elegantly.

Santa reaches to grab her arm, impatient and frustrated. "Oh come on, woman. I don't have time for your games."

As his hand reaches out, a shimmering forcefield springs up, blocking him, sending him stumbling backwards. He recoils, exasperation staining his face with an angry blush. Madame Claus, completely unbothered by his tantrums, looks up at Santa calmly. "I don't play games, that's a reindeer thing to do. But I *do* want to help you. I have a gift for you, darling. A real one."

Santa throws his hands up into the air as if the issue is officially resolved, *"Finally*, you've come to your senses. Let's see your surprise, hon, so you can go ahead and get dressed. I'm craving eggs Benedict with that homemade hollandaise of yours."

The smug way he pats his belly stirs something deep within Madame Claus. Not desire, but a raw, potent magic that rises from the depths of her being, fueled by a righteous rage She realizes that Santa will only return to his cold, domineering ways. Winter is frigid enough, it doesn't need a cold-hearted king. If Santa didn't learn what it means to serve others when he was on his knees eating pussy, then he'll need something more severe to make him understand. Madame Claus rises to her full height, shoulders back and tits proudly out. "Sylas," she says softly, "you've been a wonderful sleigh. But I think it's time to upgrade to a newer model."

She looks to Santa, her eyes gleaming with a dangerous spark. "Santa baby, won't you be my sleigh tonight, and every year, for all eternity?"

Before Santa can reply, Madame Claus raises her hands, the air around them vibrating with a potent, ancient magic. Shimmering mists coil from her fingertips, speckled with delicate crystalline snowflakes. Santa's face pales as the first tendrils of magic snake around his feet. He glances down to see his untied boots fuse together. He tries to move, but the spellwork levitates him as he reshapes into a sleigh.

The gilded cage elongates and divides his cock in two, forming gleaming runners so sharp they could skate on ice. His torso follows with the sounds of splintering wood and stretching leather compressing his naked skin, morphing him into glossy, lacquered wood. The infamous belly, so plump and comfortable, now shrinks and hollows, losing its familiar roundness. It becomes a cavity lined with sumptuous red velvet, and filled with a soft warmth Santa can no longer feel.

For the first time in centuries, Santa is truly powerless. As the last vestiges of Santa's humanity fade, the former jolly man feels a strange mixture of sensations. Some are familiar, but others are entirely new. He has an unsettling awareness, able to view the world through a three-hundred and sixty degree perception rather than through eyes or a mind. This new sense allows him to feel the vibrations of the world around him, like from the snow blowing in through the still open door. The hum of purpose is also new, like the joy of countless Christmases lives in the knots of his wood.

But his anger also lingers, a bitter ember buried deep within his polished frame. He can't shake the feeling of being muzzled. He's still *Santa*, even if he's locked in silence because Gertie didn't give him a speaker. She took away his voice, keeping him from expressing his wisdom to the world, but also keeping him from sharing his judgements. Instead, he's trapped inside of this beautiful prison, a dazzling sleigh that will sit in the garage until it's time to deliver gifts.

From across the room, Sylas watches the transformation with a mingling of awe and sadness as his friend morphs into a new form. Before tonight, he admired Santa, grateful for his role in spreading holiday cheer. But now, Sylas is grateful he doesn't have to take part in a tradition that is rooted in disrespect and exclusion.

He steps forward, his new human legs unsteady and his body buzzing with new sensations. Something feels strange, but Sylas has only recently become a person, so he can't figure out what's wrong. Although his cock can remain upright, his legs feel like they want to give way beneath him. He glances around, searching for something solid to lean against.

Sylas stumbles further, towards Madame Claus. She catches him, wrapping Sylas in a warmth unlike he's ever felt, her arms around him both grounding him and giving the reassurance that he needs to ease the discomfort.

"Come here, Sylas. You look absolutely tired," she says softly. "You've had a long night, and deserve some rest." She scans the surroundings, searching the chaotic garage until she spies the sleigh that was once her husband.

Madame Claus leads Sylas toward it, her hand steadying him as they move. Together, they climb into the opulent interior of the new sleigh, Sylas' tired muscles protesting every step of the way. The scent of fresh pine and cinnamon welcomes them, stirring up a sense of nostalgia that wraps around him like a shawl. Santa's rich, velvet lining beckons, inviting Sylas to sink into its comfort.

Madame Claus pulls a blanket over them, having found one folded neatly beside the cushions. Her hand tenderly strokes against his cheek. "You're going to be okay, I think you're just sleepy. Get some rest, Sylas. You've been a very good boy tonight."

They snuggle up together in the sleigh, sleep eluding them as the lingering thrill of arousal still courses through their veins. Madame Claus traces lazy patterns over Sylas' skin, her red-tipped nails gliding like ice dancers across his chest, down his thighs, and along his arms. Her touch is both nurturing and sensual, and the two savor the quiet closeness without any intentions but to simply be in the moment. Entwined, warm, and utterly enamored with each other.

Madame Claus' eyelids flutter and slowly close. A tender smile graces her lips as she studies Sylas one last time before surrendering to sleep. Until this moment, he had believed that the most breathtaking sight in the world was the sun rising over the Pacific Ocean after a flawless Christmas Eve. But now, as she nestles deeper into the crook of his arm, he realizes nothing could ever rival the warmth and light of Madame Claus' smile.

He marvels at the way their breath syncs, the gentle rise and fall of their entwined bodies soothing him like a lullabye. A rush of gratitude washes over Sylas, as he finally feels the type of love that Christmas is supposed to be centered around. Unconditional, and true. But even as the comfort of the season envelops him, concern crosses his mind. What will happen to Christmas without Santa? The possibilities gnaw at him, but the tug of sleep is stronger. Though he wants to wake Madame Claus and find out how she plans to bring gifts to the world, he can't. His thoughts have dissolved into a comfortable haze, and Sylas passes out.

✳ ✳ ✳

Panicked voices echo through the garage, jostling Sylas awake. For a second, he's disoriented, until he feels Madame Claus nestled beside him. Her warmth and steady heartbeat soothe him, and Madame Claus opens her eyes to find Sylas smiling down at her. The golden morning light filters in, illuminating the tenderness in his gaze.

Without breaking eye contact, Sylas leans over and places a soft, reverent kiss on her lips. Unfortunately, before they can lose themselves in each other, an elf's voice cuts through the moment.

"Mrs, Claus? Oh, thank Christmas we found you. Do you know where Santa is?"

Madame Claus pulls back from the kiss with a mischievous glint in her eye. "That's you," she whispers to Sylas.

Sylas blinks as the words settle over him. "You mean..." He points to himself, his finger pressing over the spot where his heart pounds with excitement and nerves.

Madame Claus nods. "The world needs a Santa. And I have a feeling you're going to be the best one they've ever had."

When words fail him, he leans in for another kiss, hoping that his lips can convey his gratitude. "I'm honored," he finally murmurs against Madame Claus' soft and sensual mouth. His voice is low and gravelly with emotion, "I'll make you proud, Madame Claus."

Her smile broadens, and she leans in for a

deep, passionate kiss, prodding her tongue around like a fondue poker. The moment quickly heats up as their hands explore each other beneath the blankets, the spark between them all-consuming. But the gentle coughs of the elves nearby shatter their private cocoon, reminding them that they're not alone.

Madame Claus rests her forehead against his. "I'll be waiting in bed for you to return, my darling Sentient Claus."

A wide grin spreads across Sylas's face. Once again, the rush of unconditional love and pure joy fills him as he embraces his new purpose. Inspired by his transformative night, he decides to completely redefine the traditional Naughty List. He envisions a new system, a pleasure list that celebrates writers of romance and erotica. The modern Naughty List will embrace and encourage pleasure for passionate readers. Both lists, the Naughty and the Nice, will be given gifts, but the toys will be vastly different.

Standing, he lets his rigid north pole lead the way, the mistletoe pubes kissing his inner thighs as he climbs out of the sleigh. The people on Earth eagerly await for Sentient Santa to head to work, but Sylas finds himself excited about what awaits him at home. With Madame Claus by his side, the future feels merry and bright.

# ABOUT THE AUTHOR

## Holly Wilde

Welcome to the Wilde World, where anything and everything can come alive, or just come. If you're searching to escape the boundaries of reality, then look no further. Sentient-smutty-smut and literal personification of everyday items is what you'll find under the cover of a Holly "no-explanation" Wilde book. Enjoy the ride and remember, if you don't buckle your seatbelt, your chair will do it for you.

# BOOKS BY THIS AUTHOR

## Hallowpeen

Three women, one occult ritual, and an urban legend come true are waiting for you to discover just how delicious Halloween can be.

## Airpeen

Learn about where turbulence really comes from as you share the flight with Cushy, your very own Sentient Air Chair. If you're really good, he may just invite some friends to join the party!

## Earthed

The world isn't what it seems, in fact, it's bigger and thicker than we could have ever imagined. Not to mention, it's about to explode. Celeste journeys beyond the stars and transforms into a giant woman to save the planet in an erotic story that's out of this world.

## The Deviled Egg Made Me Do It

When a giant horned (and horny) egg crashes Shelby's party, will she be able to resist his devilish charm?

## Sentient Celebrations Series

Sentient Celebrations is a series of short stories about three friends who all celebrate their thirtieth birthday together. Each special day comes with an extra special present... the lucky birthday girl gets to spend a sexy night with their gift as the objects magically come to life.

## Spf Me

These miniature men have miniature members. Just don't let that fool you into thinking they can't make a big impact where it counts.

## Taken By My Tbr

When Paige's stack of books comes to life, they make their intention clear: tonight is the night the TBR gets its finish. The only question is, will the happy ending lead to a happily ever after?

## Laid By The Lint Trap Monster

Enjoy this Quickie from Holly Wilde about a lint trap monster who is freed from the dryer, and repays the kindness with a fresh load of warm laundry.

## Getting In The Knickers Of The Nose Man

Enjoy this Quickie from Holly Wilde about a second chance romance between a sentient nose and the face he belongs to.

## Melt For Daddy

When you don't let anyone in, no one can hurt you. But what happens when an ice cube thaws your frozen heart?

Printed in Great Britain
by Amazon

51971705R00059